Dear Parents:

The **Ready Reader Storybooks**™ were created especially for children in kindergarten through second grade. This series is designed to increase children's reading skills and promote their interest in reading by themselves. The stories are enjoyable, with easy-to-follow plot structures and familiar settings. Colorful illustrations help develop young imaginations while adding visual appeal to the reading experience. Young children will be comfortable with the format and the large type.

With a variety of stories to accommodate individual interests, the **Ready Reader Storybooks**™ can help develop basic abilities and encourage your children's independent reading.

Freckles Sneaks Out

Written by Eugene Bradley Coco
Illustrated by Susan Marino

Modern Publishing
A Division of Unisystems, Inc.
New York, New York 10022

Meet Freckles.

He is a brown cat with black spots.

He lives in a big house
with many rooms…

and many people.

But today,

Freckles is all alone in the big house.

There is no one in the attic.

There is no one in the den.

What is Freckles to do?

"Maybe I'll go outside," thinks Freckles. Outside there are many things to do.

First, Freckles slides on the grass.

Then he rolls around in a big ball.

Next, he runs to the lake.

Splish! Splash! Freckles swims.
What fun!

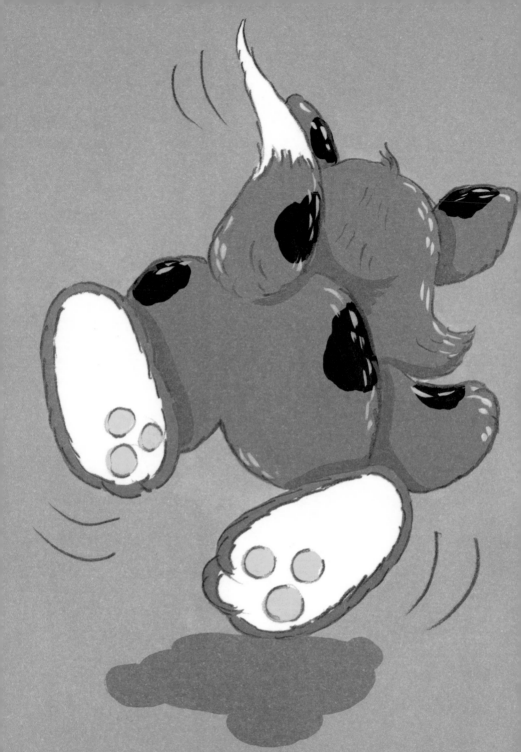

Now Freckles is off to the park.

He slides down the slide.

He swings on the swings.

He monkeys around on the monkey bars.

Suddenly, Freckles is hungry.
"It must be lunchtime,"
he thinks.

Maybe someone is back in the big house. Freckles runs all the way home.

Lunch is waiting for him.

Everyone is waiting for him.

They are happy to see Freckles.

Freckles is happy to see them.

Everyone has lunch.

Freckles does, too.

Freckles is happy.

He had fun outside.

Now he's ready for inside fun!